Text & illustrations – Minu Kim

For some time, I have created and produced many animations. After discovering the art of picture books
by chance, I decided to take part in the Sangsangmadang Bologna Picture Book Workshop.
Through my picture books I hope to bring a sparkle to a child's ordinary day.
Snail is my first picture book.

Pushkin Press
Somerset House, Strand
London WC2R 1LA

English translation rights arranged through S.B.Rights Agency – Stephanie Barrouillet on behalf of Woongjin Thinkbig Co., Ltd

Snail was originally published in Korea as 달팽이 by Woongjin Thinkbig Co., Ltd, 2021

First published by Pushkin Press in 2023

1 3 5 7 9 8 6 4 2

ISBN-13: 978-1-78269-406-9

Designed and typeset by Felicity Awdry

Printed and bound in China by C&C Offset Printing Co., Ltd

www.pushkinpress.com

SNAIL

A picture book by Minu Kim

Translated from the Korean by
Mattho Mandersloot

Pushkin Children's

"Stay here. We're too fast for you,"
the big brother said.

"I'm fast too!"

The little brother hurried along.

But on his pushbike he couldn't keep up with the bigger boys.

The bigger boys got further and further away.

"It's my brother!"

"Go back. You're too slow."

"Ugh…"

He saw a snail slowly
climbing up a tree.

The boy's heart grew light, like a cloud.

"I'll take it slow. All I have to do is keep my eyes on the sky."

Sometimes, the sky, the wind, the
grass and the trees might just tell you
something that no one ever told you.
Don't be scared if that happens,
just be amazed and happy.
It means you are a hero.

To you, the heroes of this world,
Minu Kim